The Grief Manuscript

Flash Fiction by

Frankie Rollins

Finishing Line Press
Georgetown, Kentucky

The Grief Manuscript

ACKNOWLEDGMENTS

Profound admiration and gratitude to Sandra Shattuck and Eric Aldrich,
who read through every windy disaster hour.

Love to TC Tolbert for holding down the chair in court, to Kristen Nelson
for warning me about the coming Awful, to Julia Saterstrom for practical
next-nesses, to Hannah Ensor for getting me out of the womb of the house,
to Rosie Perera for the post-it, and to Kimi Eisele for the swimming.

To these folks holding lanterns: Mary Page Jones, Bob Jones, Jill Brammer,
Selah Saterstrom, Christine Simokaitis, Kirsten Rybczynski, Dawn Paul, Sam
Bounkeua, Annie Guthrie, Hannah Levin, Julius Schlosburg, Jenna Korsmo,
Eva Hayward, Noah Saterstrom, Timothy Dyke, Cyane Tornatzky, Jake
Tornatzky, Leo Tornatzky, Raymond Rollins, Christine Rollins, Beth Laking,
Piper Daniels, Cassandra of the Five-Week House, Anthony Dee, John
Melillo and Johanna Skribsrud. The constancy of friends is inestimable.

Thanks to Leah Maines and Kevin Maines and Christen Kincaid at Finishing
Line Press for their interest in this tale.

Publisher: Leah Maines
Editor: Christen Kincaid
Cover Art: Noah Saterstrom
Author Photo: Julius Schlosburg
Cover Design: Elizabeth Maines McCleavy

For the divorce tribe

What it takes: an unhinging. An overheard conversation in a hospital waiting room, a crazy lady on a ranch, someone else's courtyard of shadows, a plague of flies in your car, a metal bed tilted in the dirt near a highway, averted eyes.

In our early days, the Right Angle wasn't only 90 degrees. He had the posture for the angle, but he wasn't only the one shape then.

The Right Angle confessed his love in front of a plate glass window. Outside, sleet poured white. I was at the end of something, something dying inside of me. The other thing died not too long after, and the Right Angle made promises.

I am cataloging slides of biopsies or resections of emotion. The tissues are thin, porous, skin-like views, golden or purple or brown. They are on wafer-thin plates of glass.

There is a photograph of us on the stairs of the first house, and Right Angle holds me tightly, as if I am a balloon that will fly away.

I am on a wooden pier above a dark water. I am walking the pier and then there are slats missing, there are holes, there are whole sections missing, and then I fall into the black, warm water, and there are others there and they slide up against me with their scales and big bodies.

My pet, Seahorse, sits on a perch in the sun. I rarely allow myself such stillness. I don't even know that I can be like him if I try. And the trying gives me away.

Right Angle is talking about fig trees. How impossible it is to rush a fig. You can't put them in a paper bag to ripen. (He dangles, bright green.)

My friend talks about her divorce, and I think that divorce is an unbearable altitude. You cannot breathe. For years, sometimes.

A windy gorge opens inside of me.

The Right Angle lets it slip that he prefers Fridays when I am not home.

It's in the attic, a sloppy, old, dusty box stained by rodent pee, the flaps torn and almost useless. It is up there with suitcases of stuffed animals and books and blankets, and there is only the small path past all the suitcases to get to the box. Inside the box, I keep a thing, an animal, that is vicious, poisonous, waiting.

I don't know how to read this book I am holding. This not-knowing makes my hands overly large, rubbery, gluey. They stick to pages, lift up chunks of paper in big spills. I want to help myself, but my hands grow larger, softer; they jelly and wet the pages.

Count up the malignancies. The petty quarrels, the irreconcilable differences. The moles, as well as the cut-out wounds from tumors, the desiccated nubs of other growths.

Sore memories can be smelled, even though it takes days, months, years to accumulate. Even the remembering makes us sink. Reverts us. How can we shed the thing absolutely?

Thank you. Sorry. Thank you. Sorry. Thank you so much. I'm sorry. Thank you. Thanks. Sorry. Sorry. Thanks. Thanks. Thanks. I'm sorry! Oh, sorry! Sorry! Thank you!

The Right Angle says he isn't sure he can get enough solitude in marriage. I think the answer is in the question. I think about finding a job in another state. I think about other shapes: triangle, octagon, circle.

I am looking for a river, resemblance, what might be hidden, what might be there, what waits to be seen. Oh! I cannot breathe! I am drowning.

The sky turns indigo before darkness descends. This happens again and again without my really noticing, because of my insides, which blind me to so many things.

The griefs are thugs. They lurk and punish. They threaten. They work out, double their bulk in no time. They gather. They loiter. Griefs that rattle in my body, tremble me with rage and misfortune. They break things, bash from the inside, fuck up my body. If I don't deal with them, they will stay. They will ruin me one hour at a time.

My heart bleeds wrong. A vulture follows me. It is always on the roof of the car, or on the roof of the house. It flaps its stinking wings.

Who am I, that made these notes?

I hold out the stick. I hold out the stick. It has peanut butter on it. I am luring the Animal out, so that I can trap it. I wave the peanut butter and I hear it rustle in the dark. Bite it, I think. Bite it with your stupid face!

I grow thorns of flesh, inside and out. They burn as well as prick. I have been let down.

The Right Angle does push-ups in the corner. 10, 100, 1,000, 10,000. He wins.

The weight of it is impossible. There's nowhere to hide it! There it is, out in the fucking open for anyone at all to see. They will see it! And they will turn away, forever.

I take a picture in the desert of a dead, dried out, standing saguaro skeleton. The way it is desiccated makes it look like a bird, makes it look split into tenths.

I look up, and my sick Seahorse looks at me, one eye squinted by the tumor growth beneath it. He'll die in one month? Two?

These panicky alone moments are new. I anxiously comb the local paper to find something "fun" to do with the Right Angle. Because if it isn't fun, then?

I believed there was another set of rules.

There are rocks tied to my spirit. These rocks have been sunk in a deep green lake. My community tied these rocks, my Right Angle tied these rocks, I tied these rocks.

Seahorse's brother, Gray Monkey, wanders the house asking questions. I answer: I don't know. I don't know. I don't know.

Part of what causes my panic is not knowing. I have this afternoon. I don't even feel like cooking.

I've been having bad dreams lately. Snakes again.

Right Angle wakes me and tells me our Seahorse isn't doing well. His paws are stained with blood. Part of his jaw is somewhere in the house, but not in his mouth. They put him to sleep. His dead mouth falls against the skin of my hand, his dead wet lip.

After a big fire, ashes float and lift on the wind. The scorch sears the air for miles. Blackness of charcoal smears what was defined, what was green, what was growing. Deep beneath, something new. Up there, fucking disaster. Between the two, only faith that growing will subsume the disaster.

Upstairs, in the attic, the box rustles. I climb up there and put a brick on top of the box, knowing there is nothing heavy enough. I knot the strings again.

The pomegranate tree leafed out in three days flat. To live so close to such perfect capability. Exhilarating.

I suffer a lack of confidence.

I put my dead Seahorse on a page, in a sentence about what I carry. *The little Seahorse's paws are bloody.* Love is like this, flashy, stuck, repetitive.

A friend calls me stoic.

I build a fragile fort out of sheets and tablecloths inside the house. They are striped, and blue and green and white. I have tacked them to the walls and the ceiling of a room we don't use. They are poorly attached. Gray Monkey and I spend hours inside. Right Angle is not interested. He does not visit.

Gray Monkey wanders the empty house, noses the old Seahorse's places. He asks his fucking questions.

There are two young stray cats in the yard. I am starving, too, so I feed them. They ghost the yard, crouch under the acacia, roll in the dirt. There is an ancient geometry of skittishness and then, endless paths of want.

I have a small surgery, which purposefully causes my uterus to die for a day. It rages out of its death throes to find blood, causes unbelievable pain. As it turns out, this is only a kind of practicing.

The Right Angle wishes I wouldn't talk in the morning and tells me so. I sew my lips shut.

Our house creaks, stinks, smokes from the ruins of our recent losses and revelations.

Maybe I want to get on my knees and pray to Jesus and Lazarus and Mary and anybody else to beg for something I don't know.

I need a sudden reprieve, a pile of kibble magically appearing in my starvation. I blink my yellow eyes.

Every time the conversation is remembered, it becomes seconded, thirded, fourthed, fifthed, sixthed, and so on.

The Right Angle measures off the spaces. He glances in my direction occasionally, but he has ceased to meet my eyes.

All of our emotions make the human testimony. Wrap it up in a plastic bag, throw it away.

Details: smoke, the stink of decay on a beach, how quickly ice melts, the moldy bread, the dirt on everything that touches the dirt, rainy leaks, silences, how love confuses self-esteem, how the distance is between people, dead birds on the beach after a storm.
I sit on the porch and think that perhaps the cost of humanity is being a part of humanity. Across the street, a lizard skitters into the weeds.

We pretend not to know each other, not to know our own selves.

The Right Angle and I agree that the most evident thing about our wedding anniversary is the death of the marriage. Orange blossom scents fill the dark garden.

The Right Angle hugs me with his emptied love and my selfhood slides away and pours out of my feet, fleeing the falsehood. It takes days to collect it all back afterwards.

I drop into the water and sink, sink, sink. At the silty, wet, clumpy bottom of the river, I come to rest. I am up to my waist in the drifty sediment, resting in furzy, yellowed water. I stare at the sheaves of light filtering down and wait.

And then, of course, the same question we all want to know of ourselves: how *does* she die?

I am in my marriage bed for the last night. There's no one here beside me. Winged creatures swoop in, above my head. They have ancestral faces, and I try to flap them away. They flap onto my table, on the chairs. They flap in the dust under the bed. They flap on my throat. They flap on my breath.

Adopt the camouflage of a weaker, smaller person. Or admit that you are weaker and smaller, and you've allowed this to happen.

As Right Angles go, this one is large and exists more as a structure unto itself than a part of a larger architectural object. Also, he wears jeans and speaks in paradoxes.

The dream becomes a fishwife, hurling crockery. Her voice is meaty and sour. The dream wears her cap and an apron. She threatens to crack my skull with a rolling pin, and I let her.

I am an albino pit bull and I've followed you home. You are kind and this makes me hopeful. I express with my eyes how much I appreciate your kindness. I thump your stranger's leg with my tail. Someone else used to love me, but something went wrong, and now I am so tired. I curl up, nose to tail, and you let me sleep.

It's a shovel in the face. Glass in the eye. That slapstick of stamping on the handle of a rake and clang! Stars, pain, but the cursing is silent because it is only between you and yourself.

It's not so much that the heart breaks. It creases. It creases and folds. Harder, and then harder still. There are hot, tight corners. Tighter. Tighter still.

I have left my pain untended, suspicious luggage in the airport. I am forced to claim it. I am forced to pick it up.

The Right Angle holds a guillotine. No, a knife. A razor. An edge that is like a guillotine or a knife or a razor.

Everything shifts and the death throes intensify. A grease stain spreads on a pristine lace white tablecloth.

It has been a while since Seahorse died. He's a little dried-up thing on the beach. Just a small, curved, yellowed, crisped spine.

If you are going to cease being a heavy, unwanted thing, there is the question, then who are you?

Other people in this store can't even smell the old man. But I can, his cells collapsing one by one on the inside. For a moment, I let my cells collapse in sync with his. Splish. Splish.

Ride the escalator down. Ride the escalator up! Ride the escalator down! Ride the escalator up! None of you, not you or the people you pass up and down, know that this was the last of joys in that lifetime.

I was already alone, anyhow.

The attic is noisy with the sounds of something trying to escape, thumping and whumping and bumping against the floor.

I close my eyes for as many minutes as I can, as soon as I am alone in the house. Not to sleep. But to not see everything.

The last string rots through. Ping! The brick tumbles off. The box, untended, disintegrates. There is a map of dried wet-nesses, a compass rose of failures. The Animal rises.

I am a woman with freckled, tattooed arms and I howl into the faces of others. They push me out of the womb of the marriage house. "Let's get the fuck out of here," someone says, maybe me.

What it is to have the daily life botched. Intentionally scrapped. Like opening a suitcase full of someone else's perfumed brassieres, spit-dried stuffed animals, sequins trailing thread.

I suffer the losses like electric shocks that make me writhe and bite through my tongue. Dark thick blood pulses down my throat, and the tip of my tongue wriggles, wriggles, wriggles loose, slips under the door.

I am homesick for the bathroom cabinet. I swear, never again.

I move to an unfamiliar street in my town. Somewhere on that street, in a borrowed house, I bring my arteries and scapula and red blood cells and eyelashes and fingertips. I try not to include the disintegrated other, but it's all over my shoes.

The onion basket in the kitchen is dead to me, too.

It's too late. The Animal is coming. The Animal is here.

Screened windows in the borrowed house, only two and a half of them in the whole joint, with gashes. I could escape.

When you let off the pressure, it slippers out: whisk, whisk, whisk across the floor.

The trees churl and wind out there, maybe a storm? In here, my footprints mark the stranger's dusty floor.

You think I'm hungry? I'm not fucking hungry. I use the butter and I chop the garlic and I cook in this cast iron pan only to gesture that I'm here. Nothing more.

In the grocery store, I am so dizzy that I have to hold onto a shelf of tamarinds in plastic jars. I whisper to myself: *Stare at this sour fruit and get it together.*

I've left Right Angle in that house of butterflies and birds and space and light across town, and I am nowhere.

The Animal inside me won't ever, ever, ever shut the fuck up. He whispers softly, *You are a burden.*

I try to eat my friends' eyes with my eyes. There must be some way to get that ordinary-everydayness, that hope, that reasonableness back into this body. I gorge and gorge and come away empty.

My key chain gets heavier and heavier. I am drowning and its weight tugs me deeper.

In movies, people try to decide whether to kill each other or not. On the news, people try to decide whether to kill each other or not. There are unbearable things happening to humans all over the world, but I fall out of the conversation.

Apparently, I bought some bacon and cut it up into portions and put it, carefully wrapped, in the freezer. I don't remember this, but the bacon is there.

In a wooden pew, I drop the false heart I've been clutching. The real heart was hidden long ago. From me? From me!

I look at an old picture and I think I am Right Angle, or I think he is me, but also, we don't look familiar at all, and I'm looking at a photo of a handsome couple on the top of a mountain in the wind.

The Burden Animal blew loose in a shower of surprising wetness, a stunning, grinning glory on his sweaty face, and now he is everywhere.

I stare at the round dome of the ceiling light in the stranger's bedroom in a borrowed apartment. Dogs bark in the neighborhood. A train goes by, relentlessly honking. I remember that something died. Something big, that once seemed to belong to me, and I cry out.

I am going to have to hang these moans out in the tree to dry every night.

The box was always too small for us. It was only temporary.

A flock of finches arrives, and I am ready for them. I have tiny missives, folded tight like seeds. You carry this away, I urge them, please.

The Burden Animal is triumphant! He is free! He has won! He was right all along! He does a jig on the bed, his fat nipples waggling. You are a burden! You are a burden!

The Right Angle shouldn't have let me get out and look back and see how any light we had was already clustered with flies.

Traps! Pouches! Pockets! Terrible ripping and shredding!

Oh! The marriage was a sham. A wet paper doll dissolves in the alley.

There are hours and days and weeks when no one can help. The field burns and burns and burns.

Sometimes people say the wrong things and it slices my brain into rings which tumble around and around and over. I chase them but often they are gone.

I can't remember what the Right Angle looks like. In a yoga class, I see a man's fingers spread on his mat. Two of them are chopped off, half-missing. Are those the Right Angle's hands, I wonder? Is that what the Right Angle's hands look like?

(I think) I have been privately shouting for years.

My friends talk to me, but I cannot hold on. I slip off the edge of the world, go spinning out into the black void. I know I can't ask them to repeat it every time this happens, so I nod my head.

From the other side of this borrowed apartment wall, I have only heard two noises: a slamming door and a waking groan.

The Right Angle sends me a beautiful lie in a note. A hammer rings inside me, slamming nails deep into boards.

The train burns through at 5 am, horn blaring the unfamiliarity of everything now. I cut off my ears and the blood drowns out the sound.

Some days it is all bravado. I flourish my new debit card from my new bank account in the new grocery store on the new side of town. I skim past families lumbering behind their heavy carts loaded with children and sodas and wrapped meat. I swing my bag and pretend that I have some fucking idea of what I've bought, where I am, what I'm doing next. La! La! La!

People tell me that it will take time. They say it so seriously, and they cannot see the hairy, segmented legs that crawl up my throat every time I hear it.

A stranger with glittered eyelids at the cash register in a pizza place looks up and sees me. Before I even order, she tells me that I must feel through the grief, that there is no way around it. She rings me up for a slice of pizza, and then she steps around the counter and holds me.

The Right Angle and I try to connect, but I slide right off the hard edges of him. I can't remember. Was I ever able to get closer?

Gingerly, I use my fingertips to feel my organs, to touch the outer edges of my brain. So many broken bits, frayed edges, blasted holes. It's all very wet, and sometimes a whole bone slides off into the dark.

You *can* be consoled, for a moment, by a perfect, warm sandwich. Just the right crunch, the right sink, the right chew. The moment passes quickly.

"Oh!" I say, sinking onto the green couch with a beer, "I really thought these days were over!" But when I turn, the Right Angle sits perfectly still on the other end of the couch, 90 degrees, no bending towards.

"Oh," I say, laughing as I land on the green couch, "My lenses were so smeary." I clean my glasses with a little disposable cloth. I say to the Right Angle, "I never bought lens cleaner like you do, you know? Just seemed like an infinite errand. But here there's plenty." I can hear my inanity, and when I look, the Right Angle isn't even there.

"Oh!" I say, bouncing onto the green couch with a cup of coffee, "It's the weekend!" But then I remember, and I stuff the coffee, the couch, the weekend, deep into the drawer with all the plastic bags waiting to be reused.

Early on, Right Angle stared at my face in bed. I asked him what he was seeing, and he replied, "Geometric planes. Circles and angles."

Humans offer solace to each other except for when they can't or won't.

Why all the sad faces? Everything is over. Stop mourning and move on. I wouldn't mind dying in my sleep tonight.

Something squeaks outside the apartment I am borrowing. Suwheeet? It asks. Suwheeeeeet?

The Burden Animal leaves a postcard with a drawing of a heart carved into right angles.

I want to snap Right Angle into a pile of sticks. Then I want to sweep the pile of him into a dustbin and throw him away.

At first, this one half a window panicked me. I was sure it wouldn't be enough. But there are leaves and shadows and birds and sky and part of a grey wooden fence, and in the distance, a telephone pole with a dove on top.

I can barely drive. I have taken the wrong turn again. My eyes are bricks, my hysteria steady but quiet, my fingers reach for nothing. I cut off my hands and crash.

I obsess about when it should have ended. That horrible fight in Cabo San Lucas? When he came back from the Maine trip? Near the otters in Seattle? Standing in the sun after therapy, the people walking by? I want a map and red pins.

The Burden Animal dances! He dances on the kitchen table with filthy feet. He bares his mossy green teeth. He breathes heavily, wheezing and banging his heels on the wood and grinning awfully. My hands, when I wash them, as pale as a corpse.

"Oh," I say, bouncing onto the green couch, "I had the worst dream last night! We broke up and I had to face my flaws, and your flaws, and suffer the end of love!" A right angle sits on the other end of the couch, silent, just two straight lines drawn on the wall behind the couch. I realize that I'm holding a pencil.

I dream of the softest places on a man's body. In my waking hours, I want rare filet of beef, poached salmon, what I can tear with my teeth.

The Animal is on the living room floor, exhaling boozy sighs from his engorged belly. His fingers are greasy and sunk in a bowl of chicken bones. He opens one eye. He winks affectionately as if to say, *I told you so, babe.*

I get a post office box, a long, perfectly square empty tunnel. Four right angles around a space. The only thing I like about it is the key.

I'll have to kill the Animal and I'll probably have to give back the kayak.

Face down on a stranger's bed, I muffle my screams with a pillow.

Fifty-two days, a deck of cards. The Fury Queen. The Lost Queen. The Gullibility Queen. Ah, there she is! The Burden Queen.

It's too much, whatever you ask. A true griever is partly dead. Go away. I can't hear you with my dead ears.

The Burden Animal screams country break-up song lyrics. He's inside me, going through me, the tunnels of my arms, the nests of my thighs, the caves of my breasts, lifting his thick leg and marking me with viscous yellow piss.

As if grief has rendered me smaller, translucent, people will not move for me in the post office, in doorways, in store aisles. They stay where they are, and I squeeze myself around them.

The Burden Animal weeps with laughter under my bed. I can hear the dry sounds of him sucking on clumps of hair and dust bunnies. He chitters happily to himself.

There is something breathing in my ear. Hot, fetid breath, rotten eggs, limburger, sweat, and I turn to behold the Animal tapping my shoulder. He winks a cold yellow eye.

On a bus in Paris, I bit the Right Angle on the shoulder. We were newly married, and I suspected that something would have to be tamed.

The Burden Animal leaves greasy smears on the furniture. He eats what no one else wants and drools while doing it: old barbecue sauce, expired yogurt, the pink spores on the ricotta.

I go and fetch Gray Monkey from the Right Angle, because I have a second borrowed house, a safe place for the monkey to come. We wake in a small bright room, the air cool. Where is the Right Angle, I wonder sleepily. Didn't he used to live with us?

Gray Monkey goes limp in the new house. He's exhausted from moving, flattened on an ottoman. I don't know if he's okay, but I envy him his absence.

I wake with a heavy, wet, sharp-nailed finger thrust in my ear. "What?" I sit up and shout at the Burden Animal. The yellow eyes blink. He belches in my face.

The Burden Animal has drunk even the lousy beer in my host's fridge. Now he licks the sticky circles on the shelves, his tongue rasping against the rippling crusted remains.

The Right Angle and I don't call. We text about logistics and it is like reading lines from greeting cards at the drug store. None of the sentences say anything meaningful or specific.

It is gagging down an ocean wave. All that salt and froth and force. I make lists and people tell me I'm doing very well.

All the fans in this house need cleaning.

I open a cabinet on my sixth day, and nothing inside looks familiar.

The discs in my back are doubling down, crunching close. They want me to run.

The Burden Animal is drunk again. His bulbous nipples rise and fall on his chest as he wheezes in the dim hall light. He's passed out on an oriental carpet, a pile of corn chips on the rug beside him, one chip clasped in his filthy paw.

There are dead bees tangled in the lace curtains. Leave them or pluck them loose?

What is that, a train nearby? Whose cup is this? Whose fork is this? Whose window is this? Whose chair is this?

I am a dust storm. I can't see through myself.

Next door, at a child's birthday party, I hear a magician with a cheap audio system. "Who wants to disappear?" he calls, in a fake-y voice. Me! Me! Me!

Take a wrong turn. Don't remember doing that laundry but fold it anyway. Find the back door unlocked in the morning. Lose the milk.

On the phone, burst into tears with a friend who isn't expecting it. Listen to the aghast silence. Be unable to stop crying. Be ashamed and yet unable to stop.

The Burden Animal is up in my memory bank, running grainy humiliation tapes. He strings images from the present and the past into a narrative of ruin and failure. The archives are endless. He's smoking under the No Smoking sign.

The Right Angle texts me about his life. Essentially, his life is a schedule. Four days a week he does one thing. Three nights a week he does another thing. He writes that he cooks on weekends. He goes to concerts. He drinks with friends. Shut up! Shut up! Shut up!

I knew his gestures, pauses, eyes, ears, neck, hands, feet, sleeping postures. This I must burn in a heap. This I must burn and cease to know. This knowing is over.

I am stuffing it down a dark hole. It's like a sleeping bag; you might think it won't fit, but I know better.

There are tiny ants on the counter, and the sugar bin is teeming with them. I thumb some to death. I close the lid on the sugar bin.

I can hear the Burden Animal looking through my papers, rustling through them. There are flies buzzing.

"Oh my god," I say, sinking onto the green couch. "Remember how we used to say that cutting someone out of your life is no good because you're always thinking of them forever after?" At the other end of the couch, a crumpled pillow, an empty seat.

The Burden Animal has spilled a jar of memories from when I was young. I am exhausted. I can't regret everything now, can I?

Walking in the unfamiliar neighborhood, I try to relax, enjoy the experience. I know none of the houses. I know none of the streets. I start to run.

At the store, pick up the roasted chickens and put them down, checking the times they were cooked. Look skeptically at the legs to see how dry they are. Put one down. Pick another up. Put it down. Carry one two steps away, remember that a single person can't possibly eat a whole chicken. Put it back on the shelf and blush furiously.

You don't know it, a friend writes, *but you're doing very well.*

I meet with the Right Angle outside, on a path in the moonlight, and I do not touch his neck or his hands or his waist or his shoulder or his cheek. He tells me lies and a small snake wriggles across the path at his feet.

Grey Monkey has gotten locked in the closed-off baby's room by accident. When I realize, he is in the crib. I rush to lift him out and he is crying, crying, crying.

A clock ticks.

Someone advises me. The advice is meaningless, and I watch a hole crack open. I see them slide in.

The Burden Animal is up in the neurons, shorting signals so that I don't know what, what, what. I get lost, bash into things, stare at nothing for long periods.

I am haunted by my attraction to Right Angle. Friends say, You've always been attracted to him. As if this is some consolation. As if I didn't know.

I will make a red jello heart mold and I will cut the desire out. No. Only the real heart will do, and the knives in this house are all dull.

The Burden Animal counts the empty chairs at the table and giggles.

I see a vision of myself, face down, floating in the pool. What a relief!

Shut up. Shut up. Shut up. Shut up. Stop thinking. Shut up. Stop. Shut.

In the middle of the night, I wake, and the Burden Animal is ready. He runs a memory film of a time I accidentally insulted a friend. I cry out, "But I never meant it that way!" He shrugs and eats a potato chip.

A friend tells me I'm grieving wrong. I sleep five hours in the day. Twelve hours the next day.

The relapse into grief space is as painful as the first weeks, which is why I pretend sternly that it can never, ever happen again. Not more than twice, certainly not.

What happens: We are rich with freedom and self-hood! We want to rejoice! We meet someone! We give ourselves away and are doomed.

The Burden Animal paces me, thought for thought. If I think, *I'm doing okay!* He says, *All your friends are sick of you.* If I think, *I'm up and this morning I feel good!* He says, *Smell the sweet syrup and see how alone you are.*

You're clipping your toenails and painting them, and then you're sobbing. The earth opens up and gobbles you whole. Soil soaks up the sobbing.

I am caught in ordinariness. The questions are much smaller than I want them to be. I am missing something.

A whiptail lizard crunches a dried June bug on the patio. I recognize the desiccation.

I dream of my Seahorse. He has been looking for me. He is thin, exhausted. I fill my hands with him.

On the phone, the Right Angle says, I don't know what will happen. I say, I think we do. The trap door opens, and I slide down to where there isn't even a crack of light.

There is a vision of the Burden Animal in my grandmother's old armchair, in another house, ten years previous. He has left a grease stain. I think, Oh, he was in that house, too? Of course he was.

I have sold a wedding ring before.

Gray Monkey is my empire, and I am his.

Call and call and call and call. The one who used to come will never come. But others will.

Get this fucking pollen off of me.

Black knots of old dream. I stuff them in my eyes, my mouth. Shhhhh!

A storm shorts out the electricity. Gray Monkey and I wait in the dark.

Jam fish spines in your throat and try to dance. Just another afternoon.

The Burden Animal doesn't realize he's awakened me. I see the white bumps of his spine bulging underneath his hairy back. Perched on the edge of the bed, he's cursing my books.

Right Angle chews rocks. Our last fight. He storms off into the summer afternoon, and then what?

I am nowhere, clutching a ticket, hoping for air conditioning.

The hours are cups in a china shop. Crash! Crash! Crash!

The suffering goes underground. What?

If you drink too much, the Burden Animal has a field day. Shows up with a trumpet, a whistle, a hammer and a pail.

Darkness like mold under your eyelids, but sudden.

The Burden Animal swirls me down the drain. A cockroach tastes my hair.

I have not forgotten how supremely delicious the love was in our early years of marriage. As soon as I have this thought, a rancid smell curdles in my nostrils. The Burden Animal's work.

Twelve movies in four days say nothing about anything. Start the next one.

Permanence flounces in, but I avoid her eyes.

In the boxes from the marriage house, Right Angle has packed me a box of tools. Go away, says the screwdriver. Don't say I never did anything for you, says the hammer. Tell people nice things about me, insists the measuring tape. The nails align to stab me when I reach in.

Undercooked. Bitter. Burnt. Slimy. Greasy. There's oil burning in that pan again, dumbass.

Another divorced person tells me how many years it will take to heal. My head falls off and rolls into a dirty corner of the yard. I leave it there.

There are bruises on my skull. I hit myself when I'm not looking. The Burden Animal shimmies his hairy ass.

Put all those kind notes in jars and throw them out to sea.

Someone confides the problems in their new relationship with me. Pausing in front of ashes where I've torn down the curtains and burned them, I nod sympathetically.

I take out my teeth and fashion them into hinges that can lock. Obviously, I cannot say.

I move again. In the new pink house, the Burden Animal changes tactics. He etches whispers into grandmother's fine crystal and smashes it on the floor for my bare feet to find in the night.

I build a small ladder; unfortunately, the screws have split the wood and the rungs are laced with thorn.

Can't I look on the bright side?

I am the horse that was killed in the making of the film. Somebody had to die.

In the mirror, a Giant Baby Head peers back at me. The Burden Animal giggles.

I dig the shabbiest fucking garden.

I wouldn't mind a darker dress, or maybe an entirely more essential and permanent darkness.

A stray cat hurls herself at our door. Gray Monkey flinches, as we've both been doing for months.

That cheap sprinkler is total shit. I stand under it, alone in the morning dirt, spattered.

I use a lot of exclamation points to reassure other people. Then I lie down on the couch and stare out the window.

So many things become humiliations. The Burden Animal shreds my pride like paper, prepares to make crafts with glue and water.

In the mirror, is there a tint of yellow in my eyes?

I used to brag to Right Angle how well-suited we were for one another. The projector whirs. I watch us pose on a beach full of colorful rocks. The Burden Animal lights up a joint.

A circular bruise on my right side doesn't go away. I wake one night to find the Burden Animal sucking there, eyes closed. I scream and shove him off, and his fat body hits the floor with a thump. A moment of silence. He laughs his wheezy laugh.

I wish I could extract Right Angle's memory of me. Then I realize that I can erase him instead. Blend him into every square thing I know.

I am going to kill the Animal. He senses it. He's gotten cagey; he hides. I can feel the yellow of his eyes in my innards.

I imagine biting the Burden Animal's fat arm and I gag on the smell.

The judge flourishes a wand and pronounces me single.

There is a flood of tears, big and heavy like cashews.

The Right Angle starts dating a friend of mine. I pretend I don't see because I don't want to eat all of this glass in public anymore.

There is a construction site across the street. I tiptoe to the yellow fence and hurl marital reminders into the mass of dirt and machines.

The Burden Animal is on center stage, spot lit. He isn't nervous. He's bursting with pleasure, each nipple casting a shadow. He looks greasy and greenish. An announcer introduces him, emphasizing syllables, "The BUR-den AN-I-mal!" The Animal grins his grassy grin and does a sort of soft-shoe dance before bowing.

Someone in the audience asks him, "Where do you reside?" The Animal points to the left side of the theatre, where I sit, thinking myself unnoticed.

Now the Animal is doing a new dance, walking backwards in a circle, his yellow eyes on me, and I realize he thinks he's moonwalking. He gives me a thumbs up.

Someone else in the audience asks him, "Why don't you just leave her alone?" The Burden Animal mimes a big box, pretends he can't get out.

Next, the Burden Animal appears beside me in the velvet seat, stuffing his mouth with popcorn. "After all," he whispers, "what is a home but something to lose?"

"Shh," I tell him, reaching for the popcorn bag. "Something is going to happen next."

Frankie Rollins is the author of a collection of fiction, *The Sin Eater & Other Stories* (Queen's Ferry Press, 2012) and *Doctor Porchiat's Dream in the Running Wild Novella Anthology Volume 3* (2019). Rollins has published in *Feminist Wire, Fairy Tale Review, Conjunctions*, and *The New England Review*, among others. She teaches honors and creative writing at Pima Community College in Tucson.

CPSIA information can be obtained
at www.ICGtesting.com
Printed in the USA
JSHW040832190520
5760JS00002B/154